For Thomas and my cats

a minedition book

North American edition published 2015 by Michael Neugebauer Publishing Ltd. Hong Kong

Text and illustrations copyright © 2011 by Judith Loske
English text adaption by Kate Westerlund
Rights arranged with "minedition" Rights and Licensing AG, Zurich, Switzerland.

Michael Neugebauer Publishing Ltd., Unit 23, 7F, Kowloon Bay Industrial Centre,
15 Wang Hoi Road, Kowloon Bay, Hong Kong. e-mail: info@minedition.com
This book was printed in May 2015 at L.Rex Printing Co Ltd.,
3/F., Blue Box Factory Building, 25 Hing Wo Street, Tin Wan, Aberdeen, Hong Kong, China.
Typesetting in Papyrus.

Library of Congress Cataloging-in-Publication Data available upon request.

ISBN 978-988-8341-00-9
10 9 8 7 6 5 4 3 2 1
First Impression

For more information please visit our website: www.minedition.com

Judith Loske
Sadako's Cranes

Translated by Kate Westerlund

minedition

Let me tell you the story of my friend,
Sadako Sasaki...

It all began on a sunny morning in August, 1945.
We were playing on the bank of the river.
We ate rice balls and lay in the grass.

We heard chirping crickets nearby.
We tried to catch them, but Sadako's tiny hands
were too slow.

Then the huge black cloud came.

It brought fire and heat, and destroyed
everything around us.
Nothing was left but gray ash.

Ten years later that cloud was almost forgotten
when Sadako became ill.

She had to go to the hospital.
The cloud was to blame.
Sadako knew it, but she was not afraid.
Her brother told her an old legend.
"If you fold 1,000 paper cranes," he said,
"you'll get to make a wish."

Sadako wanted nothing more than to get well,
so every day she folded cranes.
And though each one she folded made her happier,
the effort took a great deal of her strength.
Her family was very worried.

I lay with her and tried to hide
the fear I felt for Sadako.

ロスケ
ユディット

When she had finished 500 cranes,
Sadako hung them over her bed.

They were so beautiful.

While she kept folding more cranes, I told her stories—
stories about things I knew she loved.

Sadako, your mother will make us some delicious green tea.

We will take walks in the park, and in the spring we'll look at the cherry trees in bloom.

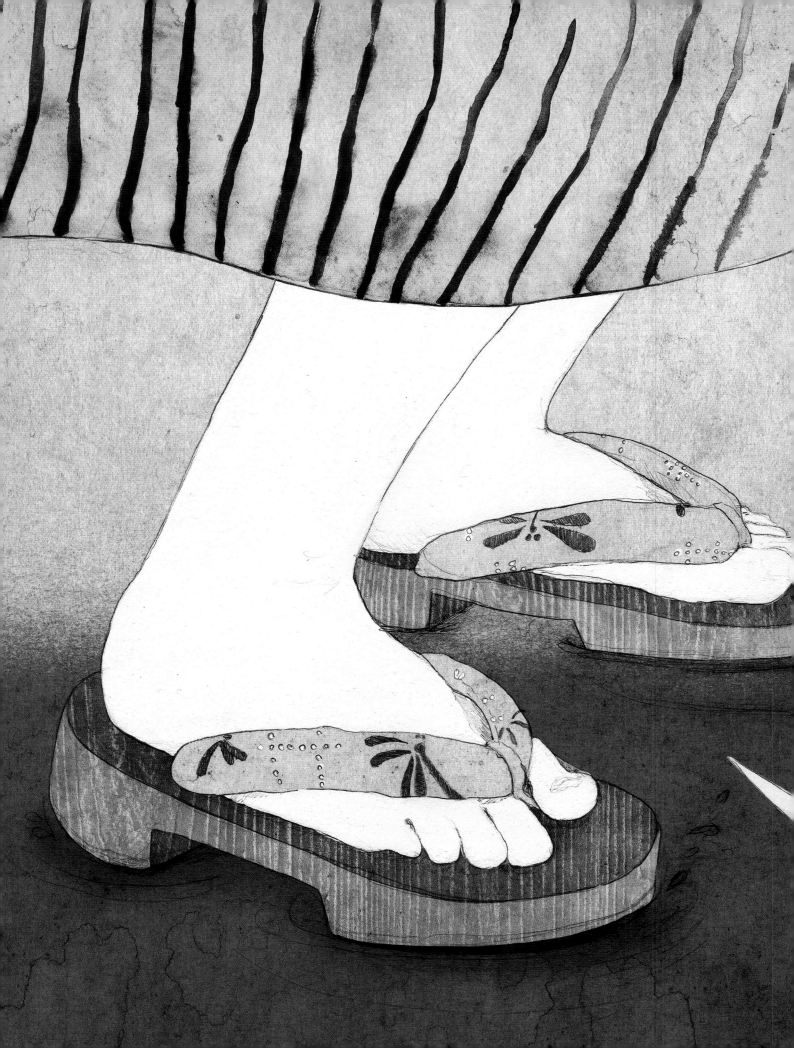

We'll go skipping through the rain,
jumping in every puddle we see.

We will travel to the ancient arch in the water.

Then we will come home on the back of
a giant dragon.

But Sadako never came home.

She gently fell asleep and flew away with 1,000 paper cranes.

I was left alone. I didn't understand why
Sadako had to die; she had fought so bravely.

I decided to do all the things
we had wanted to do together.
In my thoughts,
Sadako was always with me.

At the end of my journey, I understood
that our time together would forever have
a place in my heart.
Now I carry Sadako's story out into the world.

And I know that Sadako will live on in each folded crane.

Sadako Sasaki (佐々木禎子) was a real person.
She was born on January 7, 1943 in Hiroshima and died there in 1955. She is the most famous victim of the atomic bombs dropped on Hiroshima and Nagasaki.

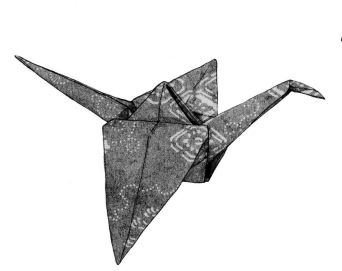

On August 6, 1945, when she was two and a half, Sadako survived "Little Boy," the bomb dropped on Hiroshima. She seemed healthy as she was growing up, but ten years later she was diagnosed with leukemia, a result of radiation from the bomb.

In Japan, the crane has an important meaning; it is a symbol of long life. When Sadako learned of the legend of the 1,000 cranes, she began folding the paper birds, hoping to recover.
Sadly, in the end, her wish did not come true and she died.
The number of cranes Sadako actually folded varies in the different stories that have been handed down.